Animal Attack and Defense

MIMICRY AND RELATIONSHIPS

Kimberley Jane Pryor

Marshall Cavendish
Benchmark

New York

This edition first published in 2010 in the United States of America by
MARSHALL CAVENDISH BENCHMARK.

MARSHALL CAVENDISH BENCHMARK
99 White Plains Road
Tarrytown, NY 10591
www.marshallcavendish.us

All Internet sites were available and accurate when sent to press.

First published in 2008 by
MACMILLAN EDUCATION AUSTRALIA PTY LTD
15–19 Claremont Street, South Yarra 3141

Visit our website at www.macmillan.com.au or go directly to www.macmillanlibrary.com.au

Associated companies and representatives throughout the world.

Copyright © Kimberley Jane Pryor 2009

Library of Congress Cataloging-in-Publication Data

Pryor, Kimberley Jane.
    Mimicry and relationships / by Kimberley Jane Pryor.
        p. cm. – (Animal attack and defense)
    Includes index.
    Summary: "Discusses how animals use mimicry and relationships to protect themselves from predators or to
catch prey"–Provided by publisher.
    ISBN 978-0-7614-4421-3
    1. Mimicry (Biology)–Juvenile literature. 2. Symbiosis–Juvenile literature. I. Title.
    QH546.P78 2009
    591.47'3–dc22
                                                                                        2009004995

Edited by Julia Carlomagno
Text and cover design by Ben Galpin
Page layout by Domenic Lauricella
Photo research by Claire Armstrong and Legend Images

Printed in the United States

Acknowledgments
The author and the publisher are grateful to the following for permission to reproduce copyright material:

Cover and title page photo of an owl butterfly © Bruce Coleman Inc/Alamy/Photolibrary

Photos courtesy of: © Arco Images GmbH/Alamy/Photolibrary, **23**; © Blickwinkel /Alamy/Photolibrary, **27**; ©
Bruce Coleman Inc./Alamy/Photolibrary, **19**; © Liquid-Light Underwater Photography/Alamy/Photolibrary, **16**; ©
Chris Mattison/Alamy/Photolibrary, **14**; © Visual & Written SL/Alamy/Photolibrary, **21**, **25**; © Kathie Atkinson/
Auscape, **30** (right); © Aegten Dominique, **6**; © Asther Lau Choon Siew/Dreamstime.com, **24**; © Getty Images/
Denny Allen, **22**; © Getty Images/Robert Canis, **4**; © Getty Images/David Doubilet/National Geographic, **17**;
© Getty Images/Mike Kelly, **26**; © Tony Campbell/iStockphoto.com, **11**; © James Knighten/iStockphoto.com,
12; © Zeynep Mufti/iStockphoto.com, **29**; © William Perry/iStockphoto.com, **10**; Photolibrary/Scott Camazine,
13; Photolibrary/Creatas, **18**; Photolibrary/Reinhard Dirscherl, **30** (left); Photolibrary/Georgette Douwma, **20**;
Photolibrary/David B Fleetham, **28**; Photolibrary/Patti Murray, **8**; Photolibrary/Nature's Inc, **5**; Photolibrary/
Photo Researchers, **15**; Photolibrary/Simon D Pollard, **9**; Photolibrary/SPL/Peter Scoones, **7**.

While every care has been taken to trace and acknowledge copyright, the publisher tenders their apologies
for any accidental infringement where copyright has proved untraceable. Where the attempt has been
unsuccessful, the publisher welcomes information that would redress the situation.

For Nick, Ashley, and Thomas

1 3 5 6 4 2

Contents

Glossary Word

When a word is printed in **bold**, you can look up its meaning in the glossary on page 31.

Mimicry................

Types of Mimicry

In most types of mimicry, animals trick predators into believing that they taste bad or are dangerous. Sometimes animals look or behave like dangerous animals so that predators are fooled into thinking that they are dangerous. Sometimes different types of animals look like each other. Predators that have had a nasty experience with one of them stay away from all of them.

Harmless hoverflies look like stinging wasps so that predators stay away.

Hawk moth caterpillars make their false eyes swell up so they look like scary snakes.

How Mimicry Protects Animals

Mimicry makes harmless animals look like dangerous animals that predators should stay away from.

By mimicking a dangerous animal that shares its **habitat**, a harmless animal increases its chance of survival. Animals that look like poisonous or **venomous** animals are the most successful at mimicry. Their appearance warns predators to stay away, so predators leave them alone.

Vital Statistics

- **Length:** 3.9 inches to 6.6 feet (10 centimeters to 2 meters)
- **Habitat:** sandy or muddy ocean floor
- **Distribution:** Pacific and Atlantic oceans, and many northern seas
- **Prey:** other fish, worms, and shrimp

Flatfish

Flatfish lurk on the ocean floor and **ambush** their prey. Some flatfish have poison glands at the base of some of their fins.

Flatfish spend most of their time lying on the ocean floor. They bury parts of their bodies in the sand and mud while they **scan** the water for prey. When **unwary** fish swim by, flatfish explode out of their hiding places and grab them.

A Flatfish's Appearance

A flatfish is an oval-shaped fish. It is pale on the underside and colored to match its surroundings on the top side.

A flatfish is an oval-shaped fish that lies on its side on the ocean floor.

Some octopuses are harmless, but they mimic poisonous flatfish in order to scare off predators.

The mimic octopus protects itself from predators by mimicking the oval shape of a poisonous flatfish.

Mimic Octopuses

D aring mimic octopuses feed during the day, in full view of predators. When they feel threatened, they keep predators at bay by mimicking dangerous animals.

Mimic octopuses are in danger of being eaten because they taste good to many predators. When a predator approaches, a mimic octopus brings its arms together to make itself look oval-shaped, like a poisonous flatfish. Then it swims like a flatfish, instead of jetting away like an octopus.

Vital Statistics

- **Length:** 2 ft (60 cm)
- **Habitat:** sandy and muddy bays
- **Distribution:** Indonesia and Malaysia
- **Predators:** fish

A Mimic Octopus's Acting

A mimic octopus mimics the colors and behaviors of many different dangerous animals, including flatfish, lionfish, and sea snakes.

A Green Tree Ant's Appearance

A green tree ant's body is divided into three parts. It also has six legs and two antennae.

Green Tree Ants

Green tree ants are large, aggressive ants. They prey on many insects that live in trees.

Green tree ants aggressively defend their nests against intruders. They are so **territorial** that some bees and wasps stop visiting trees in which they live.

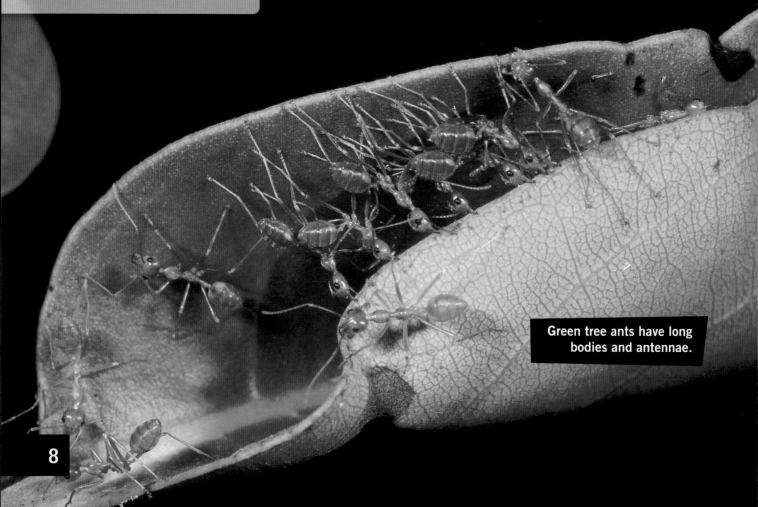

Green tree ants have long bodies and antennae.

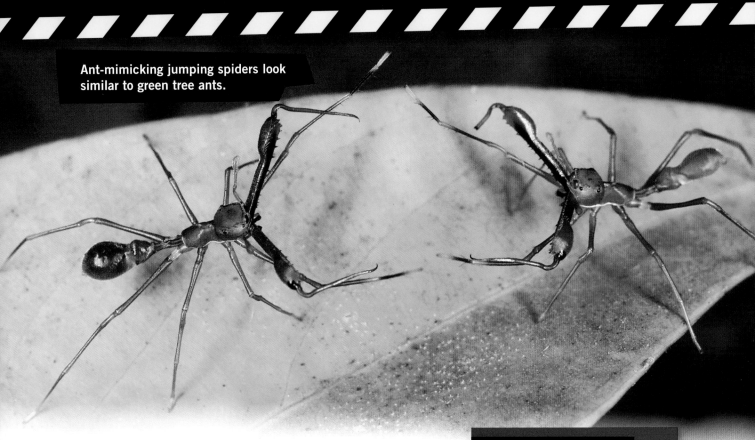

Ant-mimicking jumping spiders look similar to green tree ants.

Ant-mimicking Jumping Spiders

A nt-mimicking jumping spiders look and behave like aggressive green tree ants so that predators avoid them. The spiders and ants are often seen together in trees.

Ant-mimicking jumping spiders look more like ants than spiders because they have narrow waists and long jaws. They sometimes hold two of their eight legs up in the air. This makes them look more like ants, which have six legs and two antennae.

Vital Statistics

- **Length:** 0.3 in (8 mm)
- **Habitat:** forests and woodlands
- **Distribution:** Africa, Asia, and Australia
- **Predators:** birds

An Ant-mimicking Jumping Spider's Copying

An ant-mimicking jumping spider's body looks like that of a green tree ant, but it is divided into two parts. The spider has eight legs and no antennae.

9

Poisonous Look-alikes.....

Vital Statistics

- **Wingspan:** 3.5 to 3.9 in (9 to 10 cm)
- **Habitat:** milkweed plants
- **Distribution:** mostly North, Central, and South America
- **Predators:** birds

A Monarch Butterfly's Appearance

The wings of a monarch butterfly are bright orange with black veins. They have a black border with white spots.

Monarch Butterflies

Monarch butterflies are poisonous to most predators. Their bright orange and black markings warn predators that they are not good to eat.

Monarch butterfly caterpillars feed on poisonous plants from the milkweed family. They become poisonous, and most predators that eat these caterpillars become very ill. When the caterpillars change into monarch butterflies, the monarch butterflies are poisonous too.

The orange and black markings of a poisonous monarch butterfly tell predators to keep away.

A viceroy butterfly looks very similar to a monarch butterfly.

Viceroy Butterflies

People used to think that viceroy butterflies were harmless mimics of poisonous monarch butterflies. It has recently been found that viceroy butterflies also taste bad and make predators ill.

Viceroy butterfly caterpillars feed on willow, poplar, and cottonwood trees. In their bodies, they store an acid from some of the trees. The acid gives them a bitter taste that birds do not like.

Vital Statistics

- **Wingspan:** 2.8 in (7 cm)
- **Habitat:** willow, poplar, and cottonwood trees
- **Distribution:** North America
- **Predators:** birds

A Viceroy Butterfly's Appearance

The wings of a viceroy butterfly are bright orange with black veins, and a black border with white spots. Unlike a monarch butterfly, a viceroy butterfly has a black line across its **hind wings**.

Vital Statistics

- **Length:** 0.1 to 1.6 in (2 to 40 mm)
- **Habitat:** near flowers
- **Distribution:** almost worldwide
- **Predators:** other insects, spiders, frogs, and birds

A Bee's Appearance

A bumblebee or a honeybee may have black and yellow, black and yellow-orange, or black and orange bands.

Bees

Some bees defend their nests or hives by stinging predators. Their yellow or orange markings warn predators that they are venomous.

Angry worker bees sting intruders that try to raid their nest or hive. They pierce the predator's flesh with their sharp stings and pump **venom** into the wound. A honeybee has a **barbed** stinger. When the barbed stinger is used, it tears free of the honey bee's body and the bee dies.

The Western honeybee's colors tell predators to stay away or they will get stung.

Many stinging bees and wasps have yellow or orange markings. They look alike so that predators quickly learn to avoid animals with these colors.

An Asian giant hornet can give predators a painful sting.

Wasps

Like bees, some wasps defend their nests by stinging predators. Their yellow or orange markings warn predators to stay away.

Many wasps aggressively defend their nest against intruders. A female wasp can sting over and over again with her long, smooth stinger. When she pierces a predator's flesh with her stinger, she injects venom into the wound. The venom causes pain and may cause life-threatening **allergic reactions**.

Vital Statistics

- **Length:** less than 0.04 to 1.8 in (1 to 45 mm)
- **Habitat:** near flowers
- **Distribution:** almost worldwide
- **Predators:** birds

A Wasp's Appearance

A yellow jacket often has black and yellow bands. A hornet often has black and yellow markings.

Matching Stripes.........

Vital Statistics

- **Length:** about 3.3 ft (1 m)
- **Habitat:** forests
- **Distribution:** Central and South America
- **Predators:** birds

A False Coral Snake's Appearance

A false coral snake has black stripes in between its red and yellow stripes.

False Coral Snakes

False coral snakes are venomous snakes, but they are not deadly. Their black, red, and yellow stripes tell predators to stay away.

If it feels threatened, a false coral snake may bite a predator. The predator will become ill from the bite, but will survive. However, the next time the predator sees a black, red, and yellow snake it will avoid it. It may teach its young to avoid all black, red, and yellow snakes.

A black, red, and yellow false coral snake is dangerous, but not deadly.

14

Predators avoid a harmless scarlet king snake because it looks like a dangerous false coral snake.

Vital Statistics

- **Length:** up to 2 ft (60 cm)
- **Habitat:** rain forests and pine forests
- **Distribution:** North, Central, and South America
- **Predators:** birds

Scarlet King Snakes and Coral Snakes

Harmless scarlet king snakes and deadly coral snakes have similar patterns to false coral snakes. Their black, red, and yellow stripes warn predators that they, too, could be harmful.

A predator that has been bitten by a false coral snake remembers its black, red, and yellow **warning colors.** It avoids scarlet king snakes and coral snakes in the future, because they have the same colors.

A Scarlet King Snake's Appearance

A scarlet king snake has black stripes in between its red and yellow stripes.

A Coral Snake's Appearance

Coral snakes from North America have red stripes beside their yellow stripes.

15

A striped cleaner wrasse can clean other fish without hurting them or being hurt.

Vital Statistics

- **Length:** 4.5 in (11.5 cm)
- **Habitat:** coral and rocky reefs
- **Distribution:** Indian and Pacific oceans
- **Prey:** other fish

Striped Cleaner Wrasse

Striped cleaner wrasse scurry around other fish, nibbling at **parasites** and pieces of dead skin on their bodies. Striped cleaner wrasse do not get eaten because other fish want to be cleaned.

A striped cleaner wrasse sets up a "cleaning station" near a cave. It dances to tell other fish that it wants to clean them. Fish line up and wait to be cleaned. The striped cleaner wrasse boldly swims up to each one and picks off, then eats, its parasites.

A Striped Cleaner Wrasse's Appearance

A striped cleaner wrasse is blue on top and pale underneath, with a long black stripe. It has a small mouth on the end of its snout.

False Cleanerfish

False cleanerfish look similar to striped cleaner wrasse. They can approach huge fish without fear of being eaten because of their appearance.

A false cleanerfish dances like a striped cleaner wrasse to trick a fish into coming close to it. Then the false cleanerfish bites a chunk of flesh from the fish. It swims away before the fish has time to react.

Vital Statistics

- **Length:** 4.5 in (11.5 cm)
- **Habitat:** lagoons and coral reefs
- **Distribution:** Indian and Pacific oceans
- **Prey:** other fish

A False Cleanerfish's Appearance

Like a striped cleaner wrasse, a false cleanerfish is blue on top and pale underneath, with a long black stripe down each side. Its mouth is located under its snout.

This false cleanerfish has been caught while mimicking a striped cleaner wrasse.

17

Four-eye Butterfly Fish

Vital Statistics

- **Length:** 5.9 in (15 cm)
- **Habitat:** coral reefs
- **Distribution:** Atlantic Ocean
- **Predators:** other fish

A four-eye butterfly fish has a large false eye on each side of its body, near its tail. It protects its real eyes by hiding them with a stripe.

If a predator tries to sneak up on a four-eye butterfly fish from behind, it is fooled by the false eyes. When a predator thinks it is looking at the back of a butterfly fish, it is really looking at the front. If a predator lunges, the butterfly fish moves toward the predator, instead of away from it!

A Four-eye Butterfly Fish's False Eyes

A four-eye butterfly fish has a dark spot surrounded by a brilliant white ring on each side of its body. These spots look like eyes.

A four-eye butterfly fish is named for its spots, which look like two extra eyes.

Some animals have false eyes that mimic their real eyes. Predators get confused and attack the wrong end of the animal.

An owl butterfly is named for its false eyes, which look like an owl's eyes.

Owl Butterflies

Owl butterflies have large false eyes on their hind wings. Their false eyes look like the eyes of a hungry owl, and they often scare predators away.

Owl butterflies mimic the appearance of owls, which their predators fear. Owl butterflies flash their false eyes at predators when they are under attack. Predators usually flee in terror. If a predator does attack, it will most likely bite the butterfly's wing, not its head, and the butterfly will survive.

Vital Statistics

- **Wingspan:** about 5.9 in (15 cm)
- **Habitat:** rain forests and other forests
- **Distribution:** Central and South America
- **Predators:** lizards and birds

An Owl Butterfly's False Eyes

An owl butterfly's false eyes look very real. They look like they have a large, black pupil and a golden iris.

19

Types of Relationships

Animals form all types of strange and unlikely relationships. In some relationships, two animals live together and help each other. One animal may live near the other, on the other, or even inside the other. In some relationships, two animals live together and only one animal benefits from the relationship. The other animal may or may not be harmed.

Pearlfish sometimes live inside a sea cucumber's bottom.

Remoras can go to faraway places when they catch rides on manta rays.

How Relationships Protect Animals

Relationships help animals to find food and to stay safe from predators. Relationships can make life easier for both animals. By **cooperating**, both animals can get what they want and need.

Some animals need to be in a relationship with another animal in order to survive. A relationship can be so important that the two animals are never apart.

21

Oxpeckers often remove ticks from large mammals, such as impalas.

Vital Statistics

- **Length:** 7.9 in (20 cm)
- **Habitat:** grasslands
- **Distribution:** Africa
- **Prey:** insects

Oxpeckers

Oxpeckers are not afraid to perch on the biggest, heaviest mammals in Africa. They feed on parasites living on a mammal's skin and hair.

Oxpeckers use their strong feet to cling to large mammals. They eat flies, fleas, maggots, and ticks. Sometimes oxpeckers nibble small pieces of flesh and drink blood from sores and cuts.

The Oxpecker and Large Mammal Relationship

An oxpecker and a large mammal benefit from being together. An oxpecker gets plenty to eat and a large mammal gets rid of its annoying parasites.

Cattle Egrets

Cattle egrets strut beside moving cattle, buffalo, and other large **grazing** animals. They attack and eat the insects that these animals disturb when they move.

Cattle egrets feed on grasshoppers, crickets, and moths stirred up by the movement of grazing animals. They sometimes ride on an animal's back to get a better view. When they see a tasty insect, they dash forward and try to stab it with their sharp beaks.

Vital Statistics

- **Length:** 1.6 ft (50 cm)
- **Habitat:** grasslands, wetlands, and wet pastures
- **Distribution:** Africa, Europe, Asia, Australia, and the Americas
- **Prey:** insects

The Cattle Egret and Grazing Animal Relationship

A cattle egret benefits from the relationship with a grazing animal because it catches more food more easily. A grazing animal benefits, because a cattle egret sometimes removes insects and ticks from its skin.

Cattle egrets eat insects that are stirred up by grazing cattle.

Clown fish never wander far from their sea anemone homes.

Vital Statistics

- **Width:** up to 6.6 ft (2 m)
- **Habitat:** coral reefs
- **Distribution:** Indian and Pacific oceans
- **Predators:** fish

The Sea Anemone and Clown Fish Relationship

A sea anemone and a clown fish keep each other safe. A sea anemone protects a clown fish and a clown fish eats parasites on the sea anemone.

Sea Anemones

Sea anemones are hungry animals. They wait to sting passing prey with their venom-filled tentacles. Sea anemones also provide homes for colorful anemonefish, better known as clown fish.

Clown fish have found a way to live safely in sea anemones. They coat themselves with a thick layer of **mucus**, which stops sea anemones from stinging them. Predators of the clown fish are too scared to come within reach of the sea anemone's tentacles.

Jellyfish

Jellyfish drift with the ocean currents, trailing their stinging tentacles behind them. They are often accompanied by young fish that hide among their tentacles.

Predators that want to eat the young fish are often not brave enough to come near the jellyfish's stinging tentacles. However, jellyfish do not seem to sting the fish that hide among their tentacles. When the fish grow up, they leave their jellyfish.

Vital Statistics

- **Length:** up to 98 ft (30 m)
- **Habitat:** seas and oceans
- **Distribution:** almost worldwide
- **Predators:** turtles

The Jellyfish and Young Fish Relationship

A jellyfish does not benefit from its relationship with a young fish, but it does not get hurt either. A young fish does benefit, because it is protected from predators.

Some young fish hide among the tentacles of a large jellyfish for safety.

Some snapping shrimp and gobies live together in a burrow.

Vital Statistics

- **Length:** up to 1.4 in (3.5 cm)
- **Habitat:** coral reefs
- **Distribution:** Indian, Pacific, and Atlantic oceans and the Red Sea
- **Predators:** fish, sharks, rays, and dolphins

Snapping Shrimp

The Snapping Shrimp and Goby Relationship

A snapping shrimp and a goby help each other. A snapping shrimp digs and looks after the burrow and a goby warns the shrimp of danger when they are outside the burrow.

Most snapping shrimp dig burrows to live in. Some share their homes with small fish, called gobies, which warn them of danger.

Snapping shrimp have poor eyesight, so they rely on gobies to watch for danger. Whenever a shrimp leaves its burrow, it always keeps one or both antennae on the goby's tail. The goby uses a flick of its tail to warn the shrimp that a predator is approaching. Then they both dart into the burrow.

Feather-star Shrimp

Some shrimp feel protected from danger when they are nestled in the cup-shaped body of a feather star.

Elegant feather stars usually cling to sponges and corals. At night they roll out their feathery arms and catch food that floats past in the current. All kinds of tiny animals live in the safety of their arms, including colorful shrimp.

Vital Statistics

- **Length:** about 0.8 in (2 cm)
- **Habitat:** coral reefs and rocky bottoms
- **Distribution:** Indian and Pacific oceans
- **Predators:** fish, sharks, rays, and dolphins

The Feather-star Shrimp and Feather Star Relationship

Feather-star shrimp benefit from living on feather stars because they receive protection and leftover food. Feather stars do not benefit or get harmed.

Feather-star shrimp often perfectly match the colors of their host feather stars.

Vital Statistics

- **Length:** 4.3 in (11 cm)
- **Habitat:** coral reefs
- **Distribution:** Hawaii
- **Predators:** none known

Hawaiian Cleaner Wrasse

Hawaiian cleaner wrasse set up "cleaning stations" on coral reefs. Large fish let the wrasse clean inside their delicate mouths and **gills**.

All types of fish line up at Hawaiian cleaner wrasse "cleaning stations." They stay still and spread their fins when they are ready to be cleaned. Hawaiian cleaner wrasse nibble off parasites, mucus, and loose scales.

The Hawaiian Cleaner Wrasse and Fish Relationship

A Hawaiian cleaner wrasse and another fish trust each other. A Hawaiian cleaner wrasse benefits from the relationship by getting tasty morsels to eat and a fish benefits by getting cleaned.

Hawaiian cleaner wrasse clean inside the mouths of fish much bigger than they are.

Some Pacific cleaner shrimps even clean inside the mouths of big moray eels.

Pacific Cleaner Shrimps

Vivid Pacific cleaner shrimps are super cleaners. They leap onto large fish and give them a thorough cleaning.

One or more Pacific cleaner shrimps set up a "cleaning station" on a patch of coral or rock. When a fish gets parasites or a skin infection, it goes to be cleaned at these stations. A Pacific cleaner shrimp picks off the parasites and dead skin with its **pincers**.

Vital Statistics

- **Length:** 2 in (5 cm)
- **Habitat:** coral reefs
- **Distribution:** Indian and Pacific oceans and the Red Sea
- **Predators:** none known

The Pacific Cleaner Shrimp and Fish Relationship

A Pacific cleaner shrimp and a fish benefit from their relationship with each other. A Pacific cleaner shrimp gets food to eat, and a fish gets rid of itchy parasites.

Double Defenses

Many animals have not just one, but two ways
to defend themselves from predators.

Anemone Hermit Crab

Vital Statistics

- **Length:** 4.7 in (12 cm)
- **Habitat:** coral and rocky reefs
- **Distribution:** Pacific Ocean
- **Predators:** octopuses

Anemone hermit crabs have two ways
to defend themselves. They use their
relationship with sea anemones and
borrowed armor to keep predators away.

An Anemone Hermit Crab's Relationship

An anemone hermit crab puts sea
anemones on its borrowed shell. Sea
anemones protect the crab from predators
with their stinging tentacles. Sea anemones
benefit from the relationship too. They get
taken along when the crab looks for food.

An Anemone Hermit Crab's Armor

An anemone hermit crab finds and
moves into an empty shell. The shell
acts as armor to protect the crab's soft
body. An anemone hermit crab has
another type of armor; it has large,
powerful claws.

Glossary

allergic reactions	negative reactions in the body to some substances
ambush	attack prey suddenly
barbed	pointed
cooperating	working together
gills	parts of the body that some animals use for breathing underwater
grazing	eating growing grass
habitat	an area where animals live, feed, and breed
hind wings	the back pair of wings on an insect with two pairs of wings
mucus	thick, slimy liquid
parasites	animals that live on or in other animals
pincers	claws
predators	animals that hunt and kill other animals for food
prey	animals that are hunted and caught for food by other animals
scan	look often over a big area
tentacles	long body parts covered with stinging cells
territorial	an animal that aggressively defends its home
unwary	not watching out for danger
venom	a type of poison
venomous	being able to make a type of poison called venom
warning colors	colors that warn predators that an animal tastes bad or is dangerous